THE MIDNIGHT PONY

Don't miss any other
Young Corgi pony titles.

Also available now:

THE PHANTOM PONY
by Peter Clover

THE STORM PONY
by Peter Clover

THE SCRUFFY PONY
by K.M. Peyton

THE PARADISE PONY
by K.M. Peyton

Young Corgi Books are designed especially
with young readers in mind and are perfect
for developing reading confidence and
stamina.

The Midnight Pony

Elizabeth Dale

Illustrated by Robin Lawrie

YOUNG CORGI BOOKS

For Joan Saville
with Love

THE MIDNIGHT PONY
A YOUNG CORGI BOOK : 0 552 546836

First publication in Great Britain

PRINTING HISTORY
Young Corgi edition published 2000

1 3 5 7 9 10 8 6 4 2

Set in 16/20pt Bembo Schoolbook by
Phoenix Typesetting, Ilkley, West Yorkshire.

Young Corgi Books are published by Transworld Publishers,
61–63 Uxbridge Road, London W5 5SA,
a division of The Random House Group Ltd,
in Australia by Random House Australia (Pty) Ltd,
20 Alfred Street, Milsons Point, Sydney, NSW 2061, Australia,
in New Zealand by Random House New Zealand Ltd,
18 Poland Road, Glenfield, Auckland 10, New Zealand
and in South Africa by Random House (Pty) Ltd,
Endulini, 5a Jublilee Road, Parktown 2193, South Africa.

Made and printed in Great Britain by
Cox & Wyman Ltd, Reading, Berkshire.

Chapter 1

The smell of hot dogs drifted over, a woman on the tombola stall cried, "Have a go!" but Katie didn't stop. Instead, she rushed past every stall at the county show.

"Slow down, Katie!" her mum called from behind. "Jamie and I can't keep up."

Katie turned round impatiently. She was always having to slow down for her brother. He ambled along with his slow, lop-sided gait, leaning slightly on his mum. "But I want to get to the show ring!" she cried. "I can't miss the start!"

"You won't," said her mum. "It's only five to two."

Katie frowned, as finally her mum and Jamie caught up. Didn't she understand that she wanted to get a good spot so she could see everything?

Eventually they arrived at the ring, but there were people all round the edge. They'd come early and spread their picnic rugs. Fortunately, Katie's friend Amy had a place right at the front.

Amy waved to her. "Katie!" she cried. "Over here." Amy's dad turned and smiled at them.

"Peter? Can I leave Katie and Jamie with you?" Katie's mum asked him. "Only I'm supposed to be helping on the W.I. stall."

"Of course," he said. "Move up, Amy."

"Off you go, then," said Katie's mum. "Take care of Jamie, Katie . . . oh, and don't go wandering off."

Katie shot her a despairing look. *As if!* "No, Mum," she said.

"Isn't this exciting!" said Amy, as Katie sat down next to her. "I've been watching the horses practise. There's a beautiful grey, I'm sure he'll win."

Katie looked at her friend enviously. She had riding lessons every week and knew all about horses.

Soon the first horse trotted into the ring.

"Horsies!" cried Jamie, clapping his hands with glee. Katie smiled at him. Jamie loved all kinds of animals – as long as they had four legs, a tail and a wet nose!

The show jumping was very exciting to watch. It was wonderful to see the horses sail through the air as they cleared jumps that seemed far too high.

And they were only metres away.
Katie could hear them snort as they
breathed heavily after a jump; she could
feel the thump of their feet on the
ground. And every time they did a clear
round, she felt almost as proud of them
as their owners did.

Finally a big grey came into the ring.
And when the horse did not only a clear
round, but the fastest time of all, Katie,

Amy and Jamie clapped as loudly as anyone.

"Hungy," said Jamie, as the big horse trotted proudly out.

"Not now," said Katie.

The three winners came back into the ring, the big grey last of all.

"Hungy!" said Jamie again.

Katie clapped with everyone else as a rosette was pinned on the grey's bridle. The big horse tossed her head proudly.

"Excuse me," said a voice from behind.

Katie turned.

"That boy's pinched one of our sandwiches," said a man.

Katie's heart sank as she looked at Jamie. There was a big grin all over his face and jam all round his mouth.

"I'm very sorry," said Amy's dad. "He doesn't realize . . ."

"Hello, there!" called Katie's mum.

Katie had never been more glad to see her. One look at Jamie's face told her exactly what had happened.

"I'm so sorry!" she said to the family on the picnic rug.

"It's OK," said the man. "We didn't realize that he's . . . he's . . ."

"He's got Down's Syndrome," said Katie. They were easy enough words to say, but many people couldn't manage them. Just like they had to stare at Jamie as he walked by. Just because he looked a bit different.

"Come on, you two, let's go and see some of the stalls!" cried their mum.

Katie scrambled to her feet. She had a go on the 'hook the duck' and the bouncy castle, and two goes on the hoop-la. And on her very last throw she won ten pounds.

"Well done, Katie!" cried her mum. "What are you going to do with that?"

Katie smiled. Her eyes wandered over to the next field, where horses were already being led into their horseboxes. She knew exactly what she would do with it.

Chapter 2

"You want to spend it all in one go, like that?" asked her mum.

"Yes!" said Katie. "It will be brilliant!"

"But it will be gone so quickly. And then you'll have nothing. If you *bought* something with it, maybe a game . . . ?"

"If I have a riding lesson, I will never forget it. Never," said Katie.

"You surprise me," said her mum. "I didn't know you were so keen to go riding."

Katie pulled a face. "Well, I am," she said.

She'd longed to go riding ever since they'd moved into their house near the stables. But it had been her secret. It had to be. She knew there was no way her parents could afford lessons – not when they were saving hard for a car so her mum could take Jamie to his physio sessions.

"Oh, all right, if that's what you want," said her mum. "It's your money, after all. We'll book your lesson on the way home."

Katie couldn't sleep that night. She was far too excited. Every time she closed her eyes, she saw herself riding a real pony. She wondered if they would canter, or just walk. Or maybe trot? Whatever they did, she knew it would be wonderful.

She climbed out of bed and went to

her window. She could see the ponies in the field. Suddenly she heard a very loud whinnying sound, not from the field but much closer. She looked down.

Something was moving in the shadows in her garden. Katie held her breath as it moved forward into the moonlight. There could be no mistake. There, in her very own garden, nibbling at the lawn, was a pony! Katie couldn't believe her eyes. He was black all over, with a white streak down his nose. He was beautiful!

Katie ran downstairs. But as she opened the back door, the noise disturbed the pony. He looked up sharply and, at the sight of her, turned and galloped away down the drive at the front.

"Wait!" cried Katie, running after him, but by the time she'd got round to the front, he'd reached the end of the road and disappeared down the footpath into the copse. She'd never catch him now.

She turned and ran back into the house and upstairs to her mum and dad. "Mum!" she cried. "There was a pony in our garden."

Her mum opened one sleepy eye. "What?"

"In the garden. I saw him. A pony!"

"Oh, Katie!" sighed her mum. "You must have been dreaming. Go back to sleep!"

Katie frowned. It wasn't a dream. A beautiful pony had come looking for her, a real one. She went back to her bedroom and looked at her clock. It was midnight. She peered out of her window again, but the pony hadn't come back. She watched for over half an hour, but there was still no sign of him. Finally she went to bed. But how could she possibly get to sleep?

Chapter 3

Katie must have dropped off, for when she opened her eyes, the sun was streaming through her curtains. She ran to the window, but the pony wasn't there.

She rushed downstairs and out into the garden.

"Katie!" cried her mum. "What are you doing outside in your pyjamas?"

"I'm looking for pony hoofprints," Katie said.

"The ground's too hard," said her dad, joining her.

"So if there aren't any, it doesn't mean there wasn't a pony, does it?" she asked.

"Oh, this mysterious Midnight Pony," said her dad. "Your mum told me about him."

"He's real. I saw him."

"I hear you've got a lesson today."

"Yes," grinned Katie.

"You'd better come and eat your breakfast, then. To keep up your strength."

"I'm so excited, I don't think I can eat any," she said.

Katie could smell the wonderful horsey smell as soon as she and her mum walked into the yard. A bubble of excitement, which had been building up inside her all morning, seemed to explode as she saw the ponies again and thought that today, for the first time, she was actually going to ride one.

"Hello there, Katie!" said Mrs Finch, the owner of the riding stables. "Let's find a hat for you. You'll be riding Dapple."

Dapple was a beautiful dappled grey-and-white colour – just like a horse off a merry-go-round. She snorted a greeting as they walked over, and gazed at them with her bright brown eyes.

"Oh, you're lovely, aren't you?" said Katie, stroking her nose.

Mrs Finch tried several hats until she found one the right size. It felt strange and heavy on Katie's head, but she loved it. Already she felt like a rider.

"I've just got to finish saddling Gypsy and then I'll be ready," said Mrs Finch.

Katie stroked Gypsy. She was a dark chestnut colour and much bigger than Dapple. Then she turned back to Dapple and held out her hand. She licked it with her big pink tongue.

"That tickles!" giggled Katie.

"You obviously taste nice," said her mum, as Dapple kept on licking her.

Soon Mrs Finch was ready. She led Dapple to the mounting block and showed Katie how to climb on and then taught her how to hold her reins.

"Oh, I'm so high!" cried Katie. "Hello, Mum!"

Her mum smiled up at her.

"We'll just go in the school first," said Mrs Finch.

It was very strange to feel Dapple move beneath her. Strange but wonderful. Katie felt so proud as they walked round the ring. She could see so much more from up on Dapple's back.

"All right?" asked Mrs Finch.

Katie nodded. "It's brilliant." She reached forward and stroked Dapple's neck. "Thank you, Dapple."

Dapple pricked up her ears. And then she saw some tasty nettles by the fence and leant down.

"Oooh!" said Katie, as she was pulled forward.

"Pull her head back," called Mrs Finch.

Katie did as she was told and Dapple carried on walking. Katie grinned at her mum.

"Squeeze gently with the top of your legs and call *t-rot*!" cried Mrs Finch.

Suddenly Dapple moved a lot more jerkily. They were trotting. Katie laughed. It was amazing!

"Rise and fall with the pony!" cried Mrs Finch. But Katie was doing that already. "Good!" she said. "You're doing well."

It was the most wonderful feeling! Katie could have carried on trotting all morning. But all too soon, Dapple went back to a walk, and the lesson was over.

"How was it?" asked Katie's mum.

"Absolutely brilliant!" said Katie, as she reluctantly dismounted.

"She's a natural," said Mrs Finch. "She's got a good seat, she moves just right with the pony. Considering it was her first lesson, she did very well indeed. She could join my class straight away."

Katie glowed with pride.

"How much is that?" asked Katie's mum.

"Twelve pounds for an hour, every Saturday morning."

Katie's heart sank. She shot a glance at her mum and looked away. Twelve pounds was a lot of money.

"Well, we'll have to see," said her mum. Katie knew exactly what that meant – no. She felt tears come to her eyes and, so that her mum and Mrs Finch wouldn't see, she walked around the yard, looking at the ponies in their stables. They all poked their heads out as

she approached. Just seeing them cheered her up. Katie went round to each one, reading out their names from over their doors, and stroking their noses. None of them looked like the Midnight Pony.

"Have you got a black pony with a white streak down his nose?" she asked, walking back to Mrs Finch.

"No," she said, shaking her head.

"There was one in our garden last night. I thought he'd jumped over your fence from your field."

"He must be a really good jumper to get over that fence," said Mrs Finch. "I thought it was horse-proof."

"He ran away into the copse," said Katie. "He was beautiful. About this high with just one white sock."

Mrs Finch frowned. "How strange. No-one I know round here has a pony like that."

"Well, we'd better be going," said her mum. "Come on, Katie."

"Oh, I love it so much, I don't want to go," said Katie, reluctantly joining her mum. And then she saw a teenage girl mucking out one of the stables. It looked such fun.

"Can I help, too?" she asked, turning back to Mrs Finch.

"You'll get awfully mucky . . ."

"I don't mind!" said Katie eagerly.

Mrs Finch looked at her mum.

"Please?" Katie begged.

"All right," her mum said. "But don't go getting in anyone's way."

"Brilliant!" grinned Katie. Today had turned out even better than she'd hoped.

Chapter 4

Katie spent all day at the stables. When she got home, her mum insisted she went straight in the bath.

"You smell of horses," she said, as she ran the water.

"I know," smiled Katie. "Isn't it lovely?" She took a deep breath. "Mrs Finch said that if I help out at the stables I can sometimes ride for free."

"In that case," said her mum, "I expect

your dad and I can manage to find the lesson money."

"Really?" cried Katie. "So I *can* go and help *and* have lessons? Oh, brilliant!" She hugged her mum really hard.

"Hey, stop it! Now *I* smell of horses too!" laughed her mum.

"Oh, I'm so lucky it's half-term!" said Katie. "I can go to the stables every day."

"But I was going to take you and Jamie swimming tomorrow," said her mum.

"Jamie can go on his own."

"But he likes going with you."

"Mum! I'm always doing things with him because he likes me to."

"Well, that's what being a sister is all about."

"Oh . . . can't we go swimming later in the day? Please? I can wash all the horsey smells off me in the pool!"

"Katie!"

Katie grinned at her mother. "Well?"

"OK." She laughed. "Stables in the morning, then swimming after lunch."

Katie was very tired when she went to bed. She promised herself she would stay awake and look for the Midnight Pony. She really meant to; she even left her light on. But she fell asleep almost as soon as her head touched the pillow.

She woke with a start. A bang downstairs had disturbed her. She glanced at her clock. It was midnight!

Excitedly, she jumped out of bed and ran to the window. She couldn't believe her eyes. The Midnight Pony was back! But not only that – Jamie was down there, walking towards him!

Katie rushed into her parents' room. "Mum! Dad! The Midnight Pony's back!" she cried. "He's out in the garden, and Jamie's with him!"

"What!" cried her mum.

"That could be a wild pony!" cried her dad, jumping out of bed. He ran out onto the landing, and down the stairs, Katie following him. By the time they were in the garden, Jamie had reached the pony and was holding out his hand towards him. The pony just stood there, reaching forward with his neck, his mouth dangerously close to Jamie's outstretched fingers.

"Jamie!" her dad cried.

Both Jamie and the pony jumped. The pony whinnied, reared up, turned and raced down the garden towards the fence.

"He's never going to jump!" said her dad.

But he did. Katie gazed in amazement as the pony soared over the fence.

"Scared pony!" cried Jamie, his little face twisted up. "You scared pony!"

"It's all right, Jamie," said his mum, who'd joined them. She put her arm around him. "The pony was dangerous."

"He looked as though he was going to bite you," said his dad.

"My friend!" cried Jamie, tears running down his face. "My friend gone."

"He's only in the field," said Katie. "He's with the other ponies now."

"I think we'd better ring Mrs Finch,"

said her mum. "We don't want him jumping out again."

Katie's mum carried a protesting Jamie back up to bed, while her dad rang the stables. Katie waited anxiously by the phone.

"She and Mr Finch are going to try and catch him," said her dad as he put down the phone.

"Can we watch?" asked Katie.

"Well, all right. After all, I can't see you going to sleep until you know he's safe."

Katie smiled. She put on her dressing-gown, slipped an apple into her pocket and went into the garden with her dad.

"I can hear him!" whispered Katie.

"I can see him," said her dad.

"Can you lift me over?" she asked him. "I can keep him here until Mrs Finch comes for him."

Her dad climbed up on the rockery and lifted her up. Katie could see the

Midnight Pony properly now. She gasped. He was only a metre or so away. She couldn't believe that she was so near to him. He was even more beautiful close to. But as she landed on the other side of the fence, he started and shied away.

"Come here, boy," said Katie. "I've got something for you, look!" She held out the apple as far as she could reach, but the pony just stared at her nervously. She took a step forward, but the pony backed away.

"He's very scared," her dad called to her. "And he could be dangerous. Don't go near him."

Suddenly Katie could see lights flashing on the other side of the field. It was Mr and Mrs Finch carrying torches. They walked slowly towards the Midnight Pony. He turned and ran away from them, back towards Katie.

"Come on, boy," Katie whispered. She

held out the apple again, holding her breath as he stood there, looking at her. She could see Mr and Mrs Finch coming closer. The pony shook his head nervously. Very slowly Katie knelt down and put the apple on the grass. Then she stood up and took a couple of steps back. The pony took one step forward and then two back. He looked from Katie to the apple.

"Go on," she murmured.

He took another step forward. His ears twitched. Then, as Mrs Finch moved closer, he suddenly became aware of her. He shot her a nervous look and turned and cantered off – straight to Mr Finch. As he turned again, Mr Finch got a rope round his neck. The Midnight Pony neighed and reared up and pulled away, but Mr Finch held onto the rope. Mrs Finch grabbed it, too, as the pony reared again.

"Come on, boy," Mrs Finch said soothingly. "It's all right. No-one's going to hurt you."

He didn't believe her. He reared time and time again, neighing furiously, but still Mr and Mrs Finch kept hold. Finally the pony grew tired and, between them, Mr and Mrs Finch were able to control him. He stood there, trembling, as Mrs Finch rubbed his neck, whispering to him.

"Is he all right?" asked Katie, walking slowly up to him.

"He's very stressed," said Mrs Finch. "I think the best thing we can do is take him back to the stables and leave him in peace."

She gently started to lead the pony away, but Katie couldn't bear to leave him. She started to follow them.

"Come back, Katie," called her dad. "You can see the pony in the morning. Come back to bed now."

Katie sighed. How she longed to be able to stay up the way grown-ups did.

Chapter 5

As she lay in bed, Katie couldn't stop thinking of the Midnight Pony. The poor thing had looked so scared. Where on earth had he come from? Why was he frightened of everyone? She hoped he was happy now. He'd be lying safely in a stable surrounded by nice warm straw, with plenty of hay to eat. Surely the sound of the other horses would comfort him? Maybe Mrs Finch could keep him at the stables and she could ride him. That would be magic.

"Sweet dreams, Midnight Pony," she said with a smile, and closed her eyes. She dreamt she was riding the Midnight Pony over the hills. His mane and her hair were streaming out behind; they were going so fast, they were almost flying.

Katie woke up at six o'clock. Immediately she went to the window and looked out. An early morning mist clung to the field like a carpet, making the ponies look quite unreal. Above it, she could just see the stables. She hoped that the Midnight Pony had slept well.

Katie could hear Jamie talking to himself in his room. She went in to see him. "Hello," she said. "Today we're going to see the horsies again."

Jamie clapped his hands.

"Here," said Katie, lifting him out of his bed. "Let's take you downstairs for breakfast. Then we can get to the horsies quicker."

She held Jamie's hand as he walked awkwardly down the stairs. By the time their mum came down, they'd had their breakfast and Katie had made her a cup of tea.

"What's this?" she asked, yawning.

"We want to go to the stables as

soon as possible," said Katie.

"Horsies!" smiled Jamie.

"Oh, I was going to take you on your own," Katie's mum said.

"But Jamie loves horses."

"I know, but Jamie has no fear of animals. Look how the pony nearly bit his fingers off last night. If I take him to the stables, Jamie's likely to see a horse and go rushing up to hug its hind legs and get his teeth kicked out. You know what he's like!"

Katie frowned. She did.

"Don't worry, I've arranged to take him to see the new puppies at Mrs Kemp's at ten o'clock and then we'll go on to the stables."

Ten o'clock! Katie couldn't wait that long.

But she had to. As soon as she got to the stables, she looked for the Midnight Pony's head poking out through the top of a stable door. But he wasn't there.

Surely he hadn't escaped already.

"Hello there!" said Mrs Finch.

"Where's the Midnight Pony?" asked Katie anxiously.

Suddenly there was an awful banging noise. They all turned round and looked at a stable door. It was shaking.

"That's him," said Mrs Finch.

"What?"

"I'm afraid he's very, very nervous. He doesn't like me, or anyone else here. He's not too keen on that stable door, either," she added as the Midnight Pony continued kicking at it.

"But why?" asked Katie. "He's not a bad horse, is he? Surely he isn't!"

Mrs Finch shook her head. "There's no such thing as a bad horse, just a bad owner. I think he's been ill-treated in the past."

"Oh no!" Katie cried. "But he's so beautiful. How could anyone hurt him?"

"I don't know. The vet's checked him over. He's got a few sores – nothing that won't mend – and he needs building up. But as for what's inside his head . . ." Mrs Finch shook her head.

"Poor Midnight Pony," said Katie. "Who could have been so mean?"

"I don't know. He's not from round here," said Mrs Finch. "The vet didn't recognize him. He's got shoes on, so he's obviously been ridden before. We don't know anything about him, except his name. It's on his head collar: he's called Moonlight."

"Moonlight!" cried Katie. "That must

be from the white streak on his nose. How lovely!"

"Yes, he's a lovely pony. I've rung the police with his description and the vet's going to put a card up in his surgery to say that we've found him. But we're not too hopeful about the owner coming forward. We think that possibly someone brought him to the county show and then abandoned him."

"How could they do that?" asked Katie.

"Well, as you see, he's very nervous. Perhaps they thought he was no use to them any more and gave up on him."

"Poor Moonlight," said Katie. "Can I have a look at him? Please?"

"He's rather delicate, not a native breed, so we're keeping him in the stable at night," said Mrs Finch, unbolting his door. "We'll let him into the small paddock in the daytime."

As soon as Mrs Finch opened the

stable door, Moonlight backed away.

"Hello, boy," said Katie gently. "Don't worry, it's only me."

But Moonlight whinnied and shook his head and backed further into the corner of his stable. Mrs Finch held out a sugar cube, but he wasn't interested. She clipped a lead rein to his halter and slowly led him out into the yard, talking soothingly to him all the time, but he danced nervously about and looked as scared as ever.

Katie gazed him in wonder. In the daylight she could see him properly, and he looked more beautiful than ever. "I was hoping I could ride him," she said.

"I don't think even *I* could ride him," said Mrs Finch. She patted his neck. "There, boy." She led him over to the mounting block, but as soon as she climbed onto it, Moonlight shied and backed away.

"Oh dear! What can you do with him?" asked Katie.

"Well, we're just going to have to be very patient," said Mrs Finch. "In the meantime, we have to try to find the owner."

Katie hoped the owner never turned up, especially if he had treated Moonlight badly. "Wouldn't it be nice if Moonlight stayed here for ever!" she sighed.

Mrs Finch frowned and shook her head. "If we can't ride him, I won't be able to afford to keep him," she said.

Katie looked at her, horrified. "So what will happen to him, then?" she asked, her voice trembling.

"I don't really know," said Mrs Finch. "Let's see how he goes over the next few weeks. Maybe he just needs a bit of TLC."

"TLC? Is that horse medicine?"

Mrs Finch laughed. "Tender Loving Care," she said.

"Oh, I'll give him that," said Katie, reaching up to pat him on the nose. But Moonlight shook his head and backed away, rolling his eyes and snorting down his nose.

"I think we should leave him just to get used to being here," said Mrs Finch, leading him over to the little paddock. "There you go," she said, opening the gate for him.

They watched as Moonlight kicked up his heels and galloped around, thrilled to be free.

"Now," said Mrs Finch. "Would you like to do some mucking out? Lucy will show you what to do."

All the time Katie worked, she thought about Moonlight. Before she left, she went to say goodbye to him. She leant over the gate and called his name, but Moonlight retreated to the furthest

corner of the paddock. "Poor Moonlight!" she shouted. "I love you. Don't forget!"

That evening Katie couldn't help worrying about the Midnight Pony. He must have had an awful experience to be so scared of everyone. He deserved some happiness now, if only he would let them help him. He *had* to stay at the stables; she couldn't bear it if he was sent away.

Chapter 6

As soon as they reached the riding
school the following day, Katie ran to
see Moonlight.

"He's out in the paddock again,"
called Mrs Finch.

Katie turned and ran over to the gate.
Moonlight stood in the far corner, his
head down. "He doesn't look as though
he's enjoying himself," she said.

"He needs to get used to all of us,

humans and ponies," said Mrs Finch. "We must give him time."

Katie frowned.

"I know – how would you like to muck out his stable?"

"Great!" Katie smiled. She'd make sure she put in some soft straw, so that Moonlight would have a really comfortable night's sleep.

Whenever she had a free moment during the day, Katie ran over to the gate to see how Moonlight was. She tried to persuade herself that he was looking happier, but really he seemed just the same. The other ponies pricked up their ears when their names were called, and came over to the gate to be stroked or led into the stables. But Moonlight just wandered around his little paddock all on his own, shying away nervously whenever he feared anyone was approaching.

"Has anyone recognized him yet?" Katie asked Mrs Finch, when they paused for lunch.

"Not a soul. I'm putting an ad in all the local papers and I've made some posters, too. Do you want to see them?"

"Yes please!"

Mrs Finch went into the house and came back out with a pile of papers. Each one had a photo of Moonlight and the words MOONLIGHT. FOUND AFTER THE COUNTY SHOW underneath. Mrs Finch had described Moonlight and put her phone number for people to ring her. "All the local vets are going to have one, and the farrier and local shops," she told Katie. "It's also going up on the village noticeboard and in the police station."

Katie shuddered. That made Moonlight sound like a criminal!

"Don't worry," said Mrs Finch, putting her arm around her.

"Moonlight's owners should see it if they're looking for him. Here's a photo of Moonlight for you to keep."

Katie held it tight. She looked sadly at Moonlight. He was such a lovely, wonderful pony. She couldn't bear it if someone came and took him away. She hoped his owners didn't see the posters.

Or, if they did, that they'd realize that Moonlight was better off with someone else – someone who loved horses and knew how to treat them.

All too soon, Katie's mum came to fetch her. "You're here so much, Jamie thinks you've run away from home!" she told her.

Katie smiled. With the stables at the back of her house, she'd never need to do that! "I'll just say goodbye to Moonlight," she said.

"How is he?" asked her mum, following her. But she could see for herself. Moonlight had been near the fence but he shied away as soon as Katie approached. "Is he all by himself?"

"Yes," said Katie sadly. "It's for his own good."

"Poor Moonlight," said her mum.

Katie turned to wave to Moonlight one more time and then she went home.

As she lay in bed that night, she couldn't sleep. There was an image in her mind that just would not go away. It was Moonlight, standing forlornly in his paddock, looking so sad and so, so lonely.

By Friday Fiona and Lucy, the stable girls, and all the ponies knew Katie really well and greeted her when she arrived. From the ponies, this usually meant a welcoming whinny, and Katie made sure she had sugar cubes in her pockets – one for each of them. She always brought an apple for Moonlight but he carried on looking sad and lonely all week. He refused to take the apple from her hand, so she put it in with his breakfast.

"At least he's eating," she said, as she watched him greedily devouring his food.

"Yes," said Mrs Finch. "He's putting on weight, but that's the only progress we've made with him. I'm going to keep him in today. I want to try putting a saddle on him this afternoon, but I don't have much hope."

Katie couldn't wait to see how Moonlight reacted. Maybe he would have settled down. Everyone had been kind to him all week. Surely he would trust them now and let Mrs Finch put the saddle on him. Maybe, just maybe, she'd let Katie sit on him.

The day dragged by slowly. But finally the moment came when Mrs Finch opened Moonlight's stable door. Katie was so excited: Moonlight looked so handsome – his body was sleek and beautifully shaped, his legs were so elegant, every step he took was delicate . . . but nervous. His eyes darted everywhere, his ears twitched – he looked just as scared as ever.

Mrs Finch frowned as she bent down and looked at a foreleg. "He's been kicking about in that stable so much, he's hurt himself," she said.

"Oh, Moonlight!" Katie sighed. Why couldn't he help himself instead of making things worse?

Lucy carried out a saddle and gave it

to Mrs Finch. Slowly, gently, she placed it on his back. Immediately, Moonlight acted as though he'd gone crazy, kicking and bucking. Katie stepped back quickly, away from his flailing hooves, as the saddle fell off. Lucy grabbed hold of the rope that Mrs Finch was clinging to. It took all their strength to hold him, but finally Moonlight's kicking grew less frantic and he settled down.

"Phew!" said Lucy.

Mrs Finch stroked his neck. "Poor boy, it's all right. We obviously need to give him more time. *We* know we're not going to hurt him, but he doesn't."

Katie frowned. Moonlight must be very unhappy to be scared like that. He was so hot and he was trembling all over. Why couldn't he trust them?

Mrs Finch saw how upset Katie was. She was about to ask her to unsaddle Melody, a small chestnut pony, but then she paused. "How would you like to come out for a ride with us?" she asked. "Just round the big field. You've worked so hard, I think you deserve it."

Katie grinned. "Oh, thanks!" she said. "That would be great."

It was absolutely brilliant to be up on a pony again. As Katie sat on Melody's back, stroking her neck, she felt on top of the world. And as they walked out into the field, and she started to trot, she just couldn't stop smiling. Riding was the most fantastic thing in the world.

The next day was even better, for Katie had her first group lesson. And her friend Amy was in her class.

"It's brilliant we're together!" said Amy. "We'll have great fun."

And they did. Katie rode Dapple again and felt so proud as the pony did what she told her. She learnt how to turn her to the right and left, and how to ask her to trot.

"Well done, Katie!" called Mrs Finch as, on her command, she turned Dapple into the middle of the circle at the end of the lesson. "You're learning very quickly."

Katie knew she had to: one day she was going to ride Moonlight and she wanted to make sure she was ready for him as soon as he was ready for her.

Chapter 7

On Sunday Katie had to go to her gran's. All day she worried that someone who'd been busy that week would have time to go and claim Moonlight. And on Monday she was back at school. So it wasn't until Monday evening that she was able to rush round to the stables to check on him.

"He's still here," Mrs Finch told her as she ran into the yard.

"Great! Is he any better?" asked Katie.

"Not really. He's a bit easier to bring in, but I haven't tried to put a saddle on him again."

Katie went over to his stable. Moonlight looked out at her warily.

"Hello, boy," she said.

Moonlight twitched his ears, but he didn't back away. Katie was sure it was a sign that he was getting to know and trust her. "As no-one has come to claim him, does that mean that he's yours now?" she asked Mrs Finch.

"Oh no. The police say I have to give his owners two weeks to claim him."

"Two weeks!" cried Katie. That was far too long!

"The time will soon go by," said Mrs Finch. "Why don't you give the ponies their supper?"

Feeding the ponies was one of Katie's favourite jobs – they were all so delighted to see her. Even Moonlight didn't make a fuss when he saw his supper coming. When he was eating, it gave Katie a good chance to watch him close to. He was so sleek and handsome. Riding him would be fantastic!

By now Katie could help with most of the jobs at the stables – cleaning the tack, grooming, tacking up, mucking out or sweeping the yard. It was all great fun and, even better, it helped to pay for her next lesson.

Even when she wasn't at the stables, Katie's thoughts were filled with ponies. At school she and Amy talked of nothing else. They went to the library and took out all the books about horses and Amy tried to tell Katie everything she still had to learn about horse riding. It helped Katie to know that Amy was almost as worried about Moonlight as she was. But when Amy asked her about him, Katie had little new to add.

Each day, after Katie had been to school and then helped out at the stables, she came home to find Jamie anxiously waiting for her. He loved playing hide and seek or football in the garden, and when they'd finished, Katie fell into bed, exhausted. Each night the last thing she did was to reach under her pillow and pull out the photograph of Moonlight Mrs Finch had given her. It was more precious to Katie than anything. She could never go to sleep without stroking Moonlight's nose and kissing him good night.

Saturday was the highlight of Katie's week: not only was she able to get to the stables early enough to give Moonlight his breakfast, but she had all morning there, so she could talk to him and watch him whenever she had a free minute. And she had another riding lesson. There was nothing, absolutely nothing in the world better than being on a horse.

After riding, Katie usually went swimming with Jamie. She enjoyed relaxing in the pool and Jamie loved kicking about in the water and splashing his sister. Even when they came out, he was still bursting with energy, but at least Katie had her dad as well as her mum to play football with him when they got home.

On Sunday morning Katie got up early again and helped give all the ponies their breakfast.

"How would you like to lead

Moonlight out into the paddock and bring him in later?" Mrs Finch asked her. "He seems to like you."

Would she? Katie was so proud as she led him out of the stable. The nervous pony walked along beside her, tense but not pulling away or straining as she had seen him do with Lucy or Fiona. Katie was sure he was becoming less nervous now. Maybe he *was* beginning to know her.

But fetching him later was quite different. Moonlight did not want to be caught: each time she thought she'd almost managed it, with a flick of his head he would turn and dart away.

"Do you want some help?" Lucy called over the fence.

"No thanks," yelled Katie. She would catch Moonlight if it was the last thing she did. "Stop it, Moonlight!" she cried, as once more he darted away. "This is no fun."

But it was almost as though he thought it was. Could he be playing with her? Or was it that he still hated any contact with humans? Katie didn't know. All she did know was that by the time she finally caught him, she was completely exhausted.

"Well done!" Mrs Finch said when she led him over to the gate.

Katie smiled. She felt she deserved a medal! Maybe, at long last, Moonlight

was beginning to trust again? "Moonlight's been here for two weeks now. So that means he's yours for ever now, doesn't it?" she asked eagerly.

"Well, actually, it's not that simple," said Mrs Finch. "The police say that Moonlight has to be put up for sale at a public auction."

"For sale?" Katie cried. "But . . . but . . . that means that *anyone* could buy him."

Mrs Finch frowned. "That's the law, Katie. If I don't put him up for auction, his former owners could come and take him back. Strictly speaking, he'd still be theirs."

"But they can't! They'd only scare him again!"

"That's why it's best for Moonlight if he's put up for sale."

"But . . . but he can't be sold to someone else. He *can't*. He'd go away and I'd never see him again. Can't you buy him? Please?"

Mrs Finch shook her head. "I'd love to, but I'm not a charity, this is a business I'm running here. I can't afford to keep him if I can't ride him – if I can't use him at the stables."

"But you will be able to soon!" cried Katie. "Moonlight's getting better, I'm sure he is – he *has* to!"

"I don't know. It's taking a lot longer than I thought," said Mrs Finch.

"Then don't let's put him up for auction until he is better! You don't have to decide now."

"But in the meantime, his old owners could come back for him . . . do you want to risk that?"

"It's better than Moonlight being sold to someone who lives miles away!"

"Better for whom?" asked Mrs Finch. "You or Moonlight?"

Katie stared at her. The answer was obvious. She was being totally selfish. It was far, far better for Moonlight to go to a kind home somewhere else. But she couldn't bear it.

"Try not to worry," Mrs Finch continued. "We'll let Moonlight have a few more days getting used to us and then, on Friday, Lucy will try to ride him. That will tell us if he's changed at all."

Katie smiled at her. "Will you? Oh, that would be brilliant!"

Katie held her photograph of Moonlight extra tight that night. When she couldn't sleep, she got out of bed and gazed out over the stables. "Dear, dear Moonlight!" she begged. "Please, please be good for Lucy on Friday. Your whole future depends on it!"

Chapter 8

Tuesday, Wednesday, Thursday and
Friday dragged by very slowly for Katie.
And yet they seemed to go too fast for
Moonlight. Would he be more settled?
Would he let Lucy ride him? Each
evening Katie urged him to be good and
told him he was better now. But how
could she tell? He didn't look any
different, really, try as she might to
persuade herself otherwise. He was still

in his paddock; he didn't seem to enjoy anyone's company but his own; he would allow himself to be led into and out of the paddock, but everything else seemed to frighten him, especially people. Only on Friday would she know for sure if Moonlight was starting to recover.

Friday, when it finally came, seemed to last for ever. When, at last, Katie got to the stables, everyone seemed busy, particularly Mrs Finch. Katie just couldn't seem to get a chance to sit down and talk to her. Melody was unwell: the vet was coming to look at her and Mrs Finch was rushing to do everything else before he came. A large group was going out on an evening ride, so Katie helped Mr Finch get the ponies ready, then she watched as he led the ride out. Fiona, leading a young boy on his first ride, followed behind. Only Lucy, Mrs Finch and Katie were left.

Finally Mrs Finch was free for a
moment. She came over to Katie.

"I don't suppose . . . Lucy didn't have
time to try and ride Moonlight today,
did she?" Katie asked her.

"Er, well . . . yes, she did, actually."

"Well?"

"I'm sorry, he just can't seem to cope
with it. He wouldn't even let her get on
him."

Katie's face crumpled up. She looked
across to the paddock, where even now

Lucy was trying to catch Moonlight to bring him in, without success. She blinked back her tears.

"Oh, love, don't upset yourself," said Mrs Finch. "I'm not going to do anything about Moonlight in a hurry. For one thing, I don't even know when the next auction is. It could be weeks away, even months."

Katie tried to force a smile. No matter how far away the auction was, it was still going to come and Moonlight would be sold.

"Horsies! Horsies!" a voice called from behind them.

"Dear me, that sounds like Jamie," Mrs Finch said. "Is it time for your mum to fetch you already?" The phone started ringing, so she went into the office to answer it while Katie went to meet Jamie and her mum.

"Can you hold Jamie for a minute, love?" her mum asked. "I've just got to pay Mrs Finch for your lessons."

"OK," Katie said. While her mum followed Mrs Finch into the office, she took Jamie over to see Gypsy. He giggled with delight as she held him up to stroke the big horse's neck.

Just then Mrs Finch came rushing out of the office. "Katie, be a dear, can you tell Lucy she's wanted on the phone?" she asked.

"Of course," said Katie, putting Jamie down. "Come on, Jamie."

Lucy had just managed to get the leading rein on Moonlight when Katie called her. She tied him loosely to a loop of baling twine on the fence, before jumping over it to run to the office.

Katie stayed with Moonlight as he fidgeted nervously on the end of his rein. "It's all right, Moonlight, she's coming back," Katie said, trying to soothe him.

"Friend!" Jamie cried, catching up with Katie.

Katie turned and smiled at her brother. Even though he hadn't seen Moonlight since that night in the garden, Jamie had recognized him straight away.

"Friend!" he called again.

"Yes," Katie said, picking him up, "that's your friend."

Suddenly the peace was shattered by the clatter of a helicopter flying low overhead. Katie and Jamie looked up and Moonlight neighed anxiously. As it came even closer, the noise became almost deafening. Moonlight reared up in alarm.

"It's all right, Moonlight!" Katie said, but the frightened pony couldn't hear her. As he tossed his head, she could see the whites of his eyes.

He snorted and reared up again and, as he pulled his head back, the leading rein broke free from the loop on the fence. Quick as a flash, Moonlight raced away down the paddock. The leading rein was flying behind him, but then, as he turned, somehow it wrapped itself around his legs.

Katie watched anxiously, fearing that at any moment the terrified pony would trip himself up and come crashing to the ground. She had to get help. She put Jamie down and went rushing to call Mrs Finch, but neither she nor Lucy were anywhere to be seen. Only her mum looked round as Katie called, "Mum! Get Mrs Finch! Quick!" and then she turned and ran back to Moonlight.

Oh no! Jamie, whom she'd only left for thirty seconds, had crawled under the fence and was walking towards Moonlight. The big black pony, even more frightened now that his legs seemed tied together, reared up and twisted and turned so that he was now facing Jamie and only inches away from him. His flailing hooves might come crashing down on Jamie's head at any moment.

"No!" Katie cried. "Jamie!"

She flung herself over the fence and ran towards her little brother. Somehow Moonlight's hooves had missed him, but if he reared up again . . . ?

He didn't. He just stood there. So did Jamie. The two of them stared at each other, Moonlight breathing heavily, but otherwise suddenly, amazingly, calm. Katie slowed down to a walk and then stopped, but Moonlight didn't look at her. He didn't take his eyes off Jamie as he took a step forward and lowered his head towards him.

"Friend," said Jamie again, reaching out a hand to Moonlight.

Katie stepped forward to grab her brother's arm, but as she did so, Moonlight backed away. "Jamie!" Katie whispered.

"Friend come back," said Jamie. He put out his hand and Moonlight moved

towards him again and reached down with his nose so that Jamie could stroke it.

Katie gasped. She couldn't believe her eyes. Moonlight had never willingly come into contact with any person before, and yet here he was reaching out to Jamie. The wild look had gone from his eyes; all the nervous tension seemed to have left him. His head and neck were relaxed, his ears were pricked forward as he reached to Jamie. Tears came to Katie's eyes. He trusted him! He *really* trusted him! It was unbelievable. Moonlight reached out a big tongue and even started licking Jamie's hand! Her little brother giggled with glee. Katie shook her head in wonder. She was stunned. Moonlight was so changed: he was like a totally different horse.

The sound of the helicopter again in the distance suddenly broke the spell and spurred Katie into action. She knelt down and hurriedly tried to untangle the twisted rope from around Moonlight's legs, all the time aware of how close her face was to his hooves. But Moonlight did not flinch. He didn't even seem to notice her. Finally Katie managed to untangle the rope. She stood up, holding onto it tight in case Moonlight should try to take off again, but he just stood there. Jamie was chatting away to him and Moonlight seemed to be listening!

The helicopter came circling round towards them. Katie looked up at it, willing it to go away. If she let go of the rope, Moonlight might get all tangled up again, but if she held on, if he bolted, as he was sure to do as the helicopter came even closer, Katie would get dragged along behind him. She held on tight and braced herself . . .

But Moonlight didn't react. The helicopter started to move away and

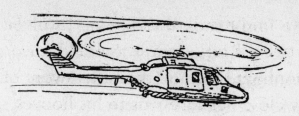

still he stood there.

"Horsie! Friend!" said Jamie.

Moonlight nuzzled Jamie's shoulder and Jamie laughed. In return, he leant forward and kissed Moonlight on the nose. The pony pricked up his ears and tossed his head, as if to say, "That was nice!"

"Jamie!" called her mum faintly from the other side of the fence.

Katie turned. Lucy and Mrs Finch and her mum were all there, staring in disbelief. Katie looked back at her brother. He was rubbing noses with Moonlight! And she wasn't sure which of them was enjoying himself more.

Finally Katie found her voice. "Come on, Jamie," she said. "Let's take Moonlight to Mum."

So Jamie took the rope and walked the pony slowly across the field towards the stunned group. Lucy hurriedly opened the gate for them.

"I don't believe it!" said Mrs Finch. "I've never seen anything like it before!"

"Moonlight was frightened by the helicopter," Katie said, as Jamie gave the rope to her and she led Moonlight through the gate.

"I know! I saw! We all did!" said Mrs Finch.

"When Jamie ran up to him, my heart was in my throat," said Katie's mum. "That horse was so wild and angry, and then Jamie — well, I don't know what he did."

"He gentled him," said Mrs Finch. "That's what he did. Moonlight was upset and Jamie calmed him. I've read about it in books — some people have special powers, they can communicate with horses — but I've never seen it. Not until today. To see that horse finally relax warms my heart." She leant forward and patted Moonlight. "What a good boy," she said.

Normally Moonlight would have flinched from such contact, but with

Jamie there beside him, he allowed Mrs Finch to stroke him.

Katie looked at her and Jamie and Moonlight. She didn't quite understand what Mrs Finch was saying, but one thing she did know: something truly wonderful had just happened. "Is that it, then?" she asked excitedly. "Is Moonlight better now?"

"Oh no," said Mrs Finch. "Calming a pony takes a long, long time. But at least for the first time I can believe that Moonlight has started to get better, and he will continue to do so until he's perfectly calm and happy again. Jamie has helped him to turn the corner. Now all we need is time. I'd love it if Jamie could spend lots more time with Moonlight. What do you say, Jamie?"

Jamie was too busy rubbing Moonlight's ears to hear her. As he moved a hand to his mouth and the big pink tongue tickled his palms, he

curled up in fits of giggles.

"I think we can take that as a 'yes'," said his mum.

"So what about the auction?" asked Katie. "Will you buy Moonlight?"

"No," said Mrs Finch.

"What? But you should be able to ride him soon, you said ..."

"I think someone else should own him."

Katie couldn't believe her ears.

"What? Who?" she whispered.

"You."

"But we can't afford . . ."

"You could because you'd be paying yourself," smiled Mrs Finch. "Moonlight came to your garden, you found him – under the law, he's yours to sell. And, after all, Jamie's the one who has started to gentle him. So you two must be his honorary owners. You both deserve him. As long as you don't mind if I stable him for you and, in return, allow some of my best riders to ride him. You, too, of course, when you're ready."

Katie stared at her. Did she mind? Moonlight was the best horse ever and Mrs Finch said he belonged to her and Jamie. Of course she didn't mind. In fact, she couldn't think of anything more wonderful in the whole wide world!

Chapter 9

That night Katie dreamt again that she
was riding Moonlight. They were
cantering over the hills, wild and free
and totally, wonderfully happy. It was
just like her first dream, only this time,
when she woke, she knew that her
dream would come true. One day she
would ride Moonlight, she knew it for
sure. And when she did, it would be even
more wonderful than her dream. She

smiled to herself. Soon, very soon, Moonlight would be happy again. Jamie would see to that. And, thanks to him, Moonlight was going to be their pony. She could hardly believe her luck.

She jumped out of bed and gazed out over the fields to the ponies and the stables. And this time, for the first time in weeks, when she thought of Moonlight, she didn't feel sad, but wonderfully proud and happy.

Jamie heard her moving around and called to her from his room. Katie went in, picked him up and lifted him up to the window. "There!" she told him. "That's where Moonlight had his first happy night."

"Friend?" asked Jamie, turning to her.

"Yes," said Katie. "I'm talking about Moonlight, your friend, the pony you're going to help get better."

Jamie didn't really understand, but he grinned anyway.

Katie smiled at him. She remembered the times when she thought that having a handicapped brother who was a bit clumsy and slow, who took up so much of her parents' time, was a real pain, but was too ashamed to admit it. But now, as she recalled the way he'd soothed Moonlight, she knew that she was very lucky that he was her brother. He was loving and enthusiastic and easy to please, unlike some of her friends' brothers. He might not be able to do everything they could do, but he could do something that no-one else could, even adults.

Katie kissed his cheek. "I'm so proud of you," she said. "You're a very clever brother."

But Jamie was still staring across the fields to the stables where Moonlight would even now be waking up. "Lovely pony," he said.

"Yes," said Katie, wiping a tear from her eye. She'd always known it, but it had taken Jamie to prove it. "Moonlight is the loveliest pony of all."

THE END